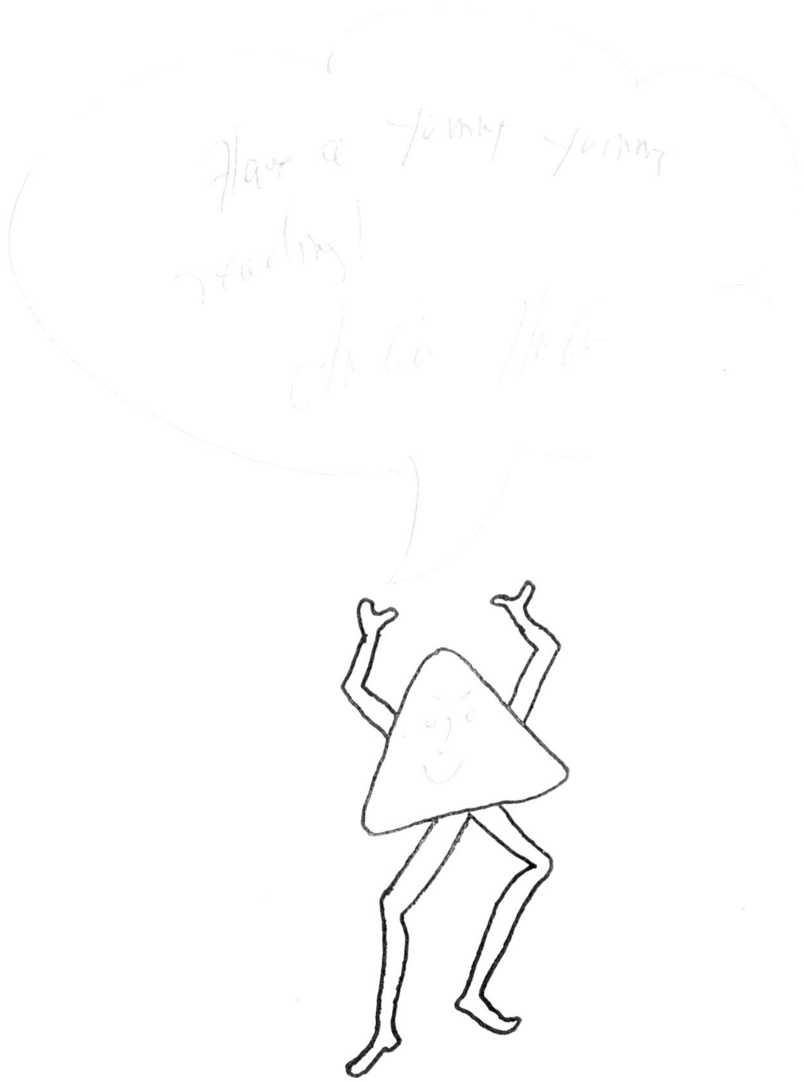
Have a yummy yummy reading!

Purim Goodies

Written and illustrated by
Amalia Hoffman

Based on a story by
Sholom Aleichem

Typesetting by S. Kim Glassman

ISBN: 978-965-229-389-3

Edition 1 3 5 7 9 8 6 4 2

Gefen Publishing House, Ltd.   Gefen Books
6 Hatzvi Street   600 Broadway
Jerusalem 94386, Israel   Lynbrook, NY 11563, USA
972-2-538-0247   1-800-477-5257
orders@gefenpublishing.com   orders@gefenpublishing.com

www.israelbooks.com

Printed in Israel   *Send for our free catalogue*

This book is dedicated in loving memory to
Tzilly and Shlomo Yoeli, my Ima and Aba.

Special thanks to Harold
for his encouragement, love and support

and to Auren and Jonathan whose
childhood inspired me.

Dear reader,

In this story you will find a few words you might not understand. These words are in Yiddish. You can find out what they mean in the glossary at the end of the book.

Zay gezunt,
Amalia Hoffman

During the holiday of Purim Jewish people send one another shalach manes. These are gifts of cakes, cookies, sweet breads, candy and fruits. The best Purim treat is called hamantaschen.

It was Purim in Stanislavka.
The sweet aroma of ginger,
nutmeg, cinnamon and cocoa
filled the streets as the town's
folks baked goodies and
prepared *shalach manes*.

In the middle of town, two girls met. They were both named Adella.

Groyseh Adella was tall with hair as black as burnt coal. She worked for Rifka, Rabbi Meir's wife.

She wore shoes that belonged to Rifka's son, Yosseleh. They looked like lions with open jaws and huge tongues.

Kleineh Adella was short with hair the color of carrot *tzimmes*. She worked for Beila, wife of Rabbi Menasheh. She wore a worn-out coat that belonged to Beila's mother-in-law. Its lining was torn and dragged on the pavement like soggy, overcooked *lokshen*.

Both girls were carrying *shalach manes*.

"Why, I am going to your house," said Groyseh Adella.

"And I am going to yours," said Kleineh Adella.

That's a good joke!

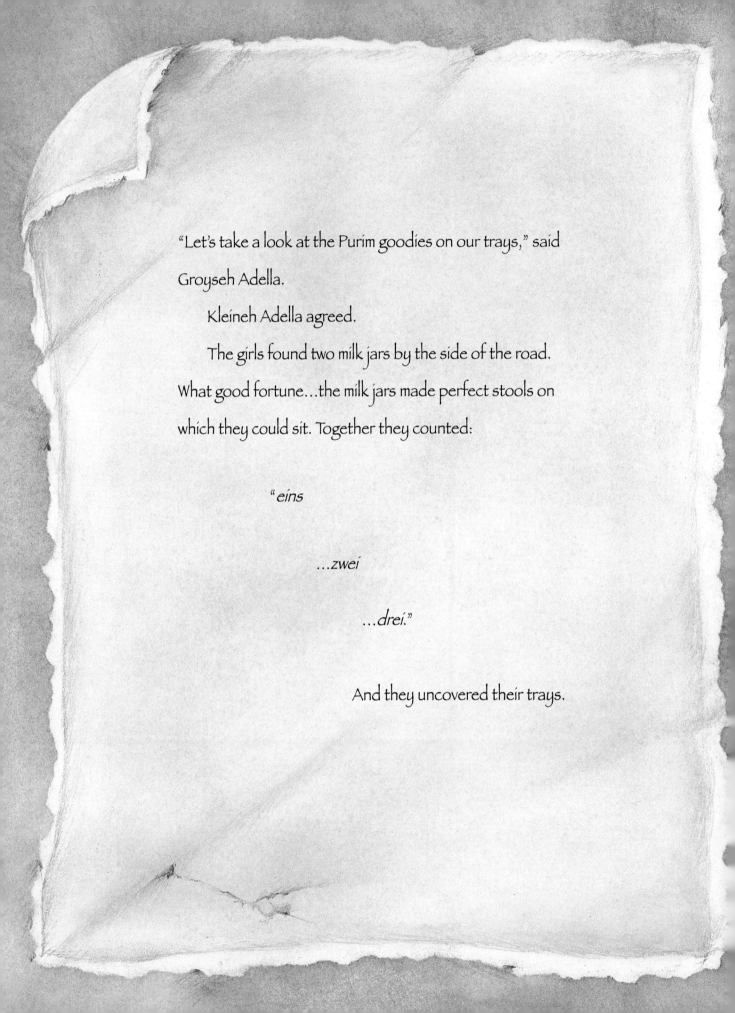

"Let's take a look at the Purim goodies on our trays," said
Groyseh Adella.

Kleineh Adella agreed.

The girls found two milk jars by the side of the road.
What good fortune…the milk jars made perfect stools on
which they could sit. Together they counted:

"*eins*

…*zwei*

…*drei.*"

And they uncovered their trays.

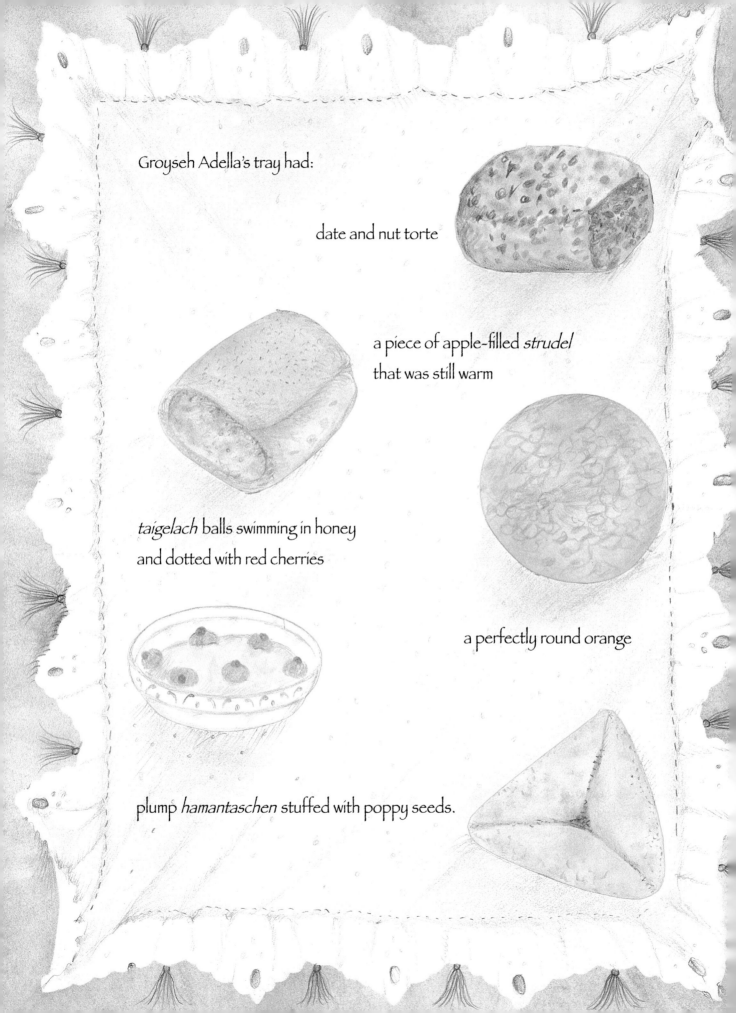

Groyseh Adella's tray had:

date and nut torte

a piece of apple-filled *strudel*
that was still warm

taigelach balls swimming in honey
and dotted with red cherries

a perfectly round orange

plump *hamantaschen* stuffed with poppy seeds.

Kleineh Adella's tray had:

kindl that looked like a baby
wrapped in a blanket

mandelbrot decorated with almonds –
sliced thin

a dish of rice pudding
that looked like a puffy cloud

an apple that smelled very sweet

golden *hamantaschen* filled with sweet prunes.

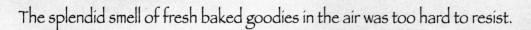

The splendid smell of fresh baked goodies in the air was too hard to resist.

"How about a *bissel* taste," said Groyseh Adella.

"Well...a *shtikaleh*," agreed Kleineh Adella. "They'll never notice."

She pinched some crumbs off the warm, moist strudel.

"Ahh – *mechayeh*," she said.

Groyseh Adella stuck her finger in the *taigelach* and licked the golden honey.

   "Ahh, this is what they must be serving to *tzadiks* in *Gan Eden*," she whispered while the

honey dripped down her chin.

And so they nibbled on the torte,

dipped into the pudding,

pinched the *mandelbrot*

and…

even though they didn't mean to…

completely gobbled up the *hamantaschen*.

"*Oy vey*, it's getting late," said Groyseh Adella. "I must hurry over to your house."

"And I must run off to yours," said Kleineh Adella.

Each walked the opposite way.

Children, there are plenty of crumbs for all of you!

Groyseh Adella knocked on Beila and Rabbi Menasheh's door. "A *gitten* Purim," she said. Beila put the tray on the table. "Oh, that Rifka – such a *balabusteh*. Last year her honey cake was so delish…" Her plump face turned red as she lifted the napkin off the tray.

That sly Rifka…she's making a laughingstock out of me!

Meanwhile, Kleineh Adella had just walked into Rifka and Rabbi Meir's house…

On *Shabbes*, in synagogue the two *mishpuchehs* were not talking to each other.

That made the rabbi wonder...and so he invited everybody to his house.

Rifka screamed, "What *chutzpah*! I'd rather eat hay than leftovers off a tray."

Beila cried, "Lies, lies, *oy vey, oy vey*; it was I who got the half-empty tray."

The rabbi nodded his head to the left, then to the right, he ran his fingers through his beard and said, "In our town there are people who go to sleep without supper and you are arguing over *strudel*, *taigelach* and *hamantaschen*?"

The two couples felt ashamed.

   They realized how silly and selfish they had been.

   They hugged and made up and quietly walked back

to their homes.

And the two Adellas?

Well, they felt sorry for all the trouble they had caused
and admitted what they had done.

And then...stayed up the whole night and baked
hamantaschen for all the poor folks in Stanislavka.

Hamantaschen Recipe

Dough

2 1/2 cups all-purpose flour
1/2 cup granulated sugar
1 teaspoon baking powder
3/4 cup butter or margarine
1 teaspoon grated lemon peel
1/2 teaspoon vanilla extract
2 eggs

Filling

Find your favorite filling on Kleineh and Groyseh Adella's aprons.

Mix flour, sugar and baking powder in large bowl. Cut in butter, using pastry blender or crisscrossing 2 knives, until mixture resembles fine crumbs. Mix lemon peel, vanilla extract and eggs. Stir into flour mixture until dough forms a ball. (Use hands to mix all ingredients if necessary; add up to 1/4 cup additional flour if dough is too sticky to handle.) Cover and refrigerate about 2 hours or until firm.

Preheat oven to 350 degrees F.

Roll half of dough at a time 1/8 inch thick on lightly floured cloth-covered surface. Cut into 3-inch rounds using a cup. Spoon 1 level teaspoon filling onto each round. Bring up 3 sides, using metal spatula to lift, to form triangle around filling. Pinch edges together firmly. Place about 2 inches apart on ungreased cookie sheet. Bake 12 to 15 minutes or until light brown. Immediately remove from cookie sheet to wire rack.

Yield: 48 cookies (1 per serving)

Prune Filling

1 cup prune butter (lekvar)

1/2 cup shelled walnuts

1/4 cup unseasoned bread crumbs

juice and peel of 1 lemon

In food processor chop walnuts until fine.

Now mix all ingredients together in bowl.

Poppy Seed Filling

1 cup poppy seeds

1/4 cup walnut pieces

1/3 cup sugar

1 tablespoon butter or margarine

1 tablespoon honey

1 teaspoon lemon juice

1 egg white

Place all ingredients in blender or food processor.

Cover and blend until smooth.

Afterword

Purim is one of the most joyous holidays and is celebrated during the Jewish month of Adar which usually falls in March. The heroes are Queen Esther and her wise uncle Mordechai. The villain is Haman, the advisor of Achashverosh (also known as Ahasuerus), king of Persia. Haman plotted an evil decree against the Jews but beautiful Esther persuaded the king not to harm them.

To celebrate the occasion, people send food packages to friends and to the poor (*shalach manes*).The Book of Esther (*Megillat Esther*) is read in synagogue to the accompaniment of much noisemaking to drown out the name of Haman. Children are particularly fond of Purim because of the tradition of dressing up in costumes and masks during the holiday.

Glossary

balabusteh – accomplished homemaker

bissel – a little, a bit

chutzpah – audacity / nerve

eins, zwei, drei – one, two, three

Gan Eden – the Garden of Eden

Gitten Purim – Good Purim

groyseh – big

hamantaschen – "Haman's pockets"; triangular filled cookies named for the villain of the Purim story, the wicked Haman

kindl – Viennese Purim pastry with poppy-seed filling; similar to *hamantaschen*, but the dough is rolled around the filling so it looks like a baby wrapped in a blanket in memory of Haman's offspring

kleineh – small

lokshen – noodles

mandelbrot – biscotti-like cookie

mechayeh – heavenly

mishpuchehs – families

oy vey – alas

Shabbes – the Sabbath

shalach manes – gifts of food, from the Hebrew *mishloach manot*, meaning "sending portions"

shtikaleh – a little piece

strudel – pastry filled with apples and cinnamon or *mon* (poppy seeds)

taigelach – dough balls in honey and sugar syrup

tzadiks – righteous people

tzimmes – sweet cooked dish made from carrots

zay gezunt – be well

About the Author and Illustrator

Amalia Hoffman has exhibited widely in galleries and museums throughout the United States. Her intricate artwork has been featured in New York City's most prestigious stores where she created innovative window displays.

Most recently, she illustrated *Friday Night with the Pope* by Jacques J.M. Shore.

She is a recipient of the *Society of Children's Book Writers and Illustrators* 2005 Portfolio award in the category of Fantasy.

Amalia grew up in Jerusalem, Israel, and celebrated Purim each year wearing a different costume.

Nowadays she lives and works in Larchmont, New York, where she spends Purim with family, friends and lots of *hamantaschen*.

Amalia (center) as Queen Esther with her sisters and parents
(Mom sewed all the costumes).